TOWN AND COUNTRY PUBLIC LIBRARY DISTRICT
3 2990 00048 1899
W9-BWU-523

Town and Country
Public Library District
Given by the
Friends of the Library

For Cugina:
If our needles could talk,
what yarns they would tell.

—E.W.

To Anastasia Chaadaeva

—B.I.

The First Christmas Stocking

Elizabeth Winthrop

Illustrated by Bagram Ibatoulline

DELACORTE PRESS

LONG, LONG AGO in the north country, a young girl named Claire lived with her mother and father. The family was poor and dwelled in the lowest valley of the town where the streets twisted and turned between dank stone huts.

Claire's father worked in the mines, and when he walked through the door at the end of the day, the coal dust had turned his skin as black as the night that brought him home. Claire's mother was a knitter, famous for miles around. The rich people who lived at the top of the town brought her wool of all colors and weights, and she made hats for round-headed children and waistcoats for portly bankers and gloves for dainty-fingered ladies. All day long, Claire's mother knit.

Because the sun rarely found its way to their door, they lived out their days in eternal dusk. They could not afford to waste candles or firewood, so Claire's mother knit in the dark, while Claire sat at her feet and played with the skeins of wool. When the child grew restless, her mother would pull Claire into her lap, tuck her cold feet into the folds of her dress, and continue to rock and knit. Claire would be lulled to sleep by the beat of her mother's heart and the slip and click of the needles.

One day when Claire was old enough, her mother wrapped her fingers around the needles.

"Close your eyes, my child. Dream your dreams and knit them into the wool."

Claire could feel her mother's warm hands over hers. With their fingers braided together, the mother and daughter wound the wool around the points of the needles and slid the stitches from one side to the other.

"Now, my child, what shall you make with your wool?"

"I shall make stockings," said Claire. "To keep my toes warm."

In the weeks before Christmas, Claire's mother was busier than ever. The rich people brought baskets of wool to the tiny house at the bottom of the lane. They ordered hats and mittens and scarves and vests. And when the people saw the stockings Claire had knit hanging above the hearth, they said, "Oh yes, I'll have a pair of those, too." So Claire and her mother knit side by side, day after day, in the deepening darkness.

The knitting was sold, and on Christmas Day, Claire's mother made currant cakes and spiced cider, and her father burned an enormous log all the day long, so that Claire's toes at last were warm and the walls of their little room danced with light.

Claire's mother laughed, and the church bells rang, until Claire did not know which glorious sound came from outside the windows and which came from inside her heart.

As the year turned and the days grew colder, Claire's mother began to cough. Soon she could not lift her head from the bed. Claire's father ran for the doctor, but he would not come to the lowest valley of the town. All night long, Claire heard the whisper of her father's voice and the low moans from her mother, until at last the girl fell into a fitful sleep. In the morning, she woke to silence.

They buried her mother, and the next day, Claire's father went back to the mines. Now it fell upon Claire to cook the meals and keep house. It was a lonely life even in the best of times, and the days dragged on.

The winter months were the hardest. Claire's only consolation was to crawl into the rocking chair, close her eyes, and pick up her needles. Then she could feel her mother's warm hands over hers, and she could hear her mother's voice in her ear.

"Dream your dreams, my child, and knit them into the wool."

Claire would rock and dream while her fingers flew back and forth, back and forth between the needles. And everything she dreamed, she knit into her stockings. The townspeople began to call Claire the stocking girl. It was said that her stockings were uncommonly warm and that she had learned from her mother how to paint pictures with wool.

One afternoon, there came a knock at Claire's door. She opened it to find a tall, thin-lipped lady with her skirts lifted high above the mud of the doorsill. Behind her stood a servant girl, clutching two baskets in one hand and the back of her lady's skirt in the other.

"Are you the stocking girl?" the lady asked.

"That I am," said Claire.

"I want you to make stockings for my three children for Christmas. I have brought the wool." The lady snatched the baskets from her servant girl and thrust them into Claire's hands.

"But Christmas is only two days hence," Claire said.

"I shall pay handsomely," the lady said. "I live in the red house at the very top of the lane. It is the biggest house in all the town, so you shall know it when you see it. You must deliver the six stockings to me by six o'clock on Christmas Eve."

"I shall try, ma'am," Claire said, although she wondered how she could possibly knit six whole stockings by the day after next.

Without another word, the haughty lady made her way back up the muddy lane, while the servant girl skittered along behind, lifting her ladyship's skirts this way and that.

Claire sat down that very minute and set to work. When her father opened the door, she was bowed over the wool with her eyes closed and her fingers dancing up and down the wooden needles.

"Father!" Claire cried. "I am to knit six stockings by Christmas Eve for a rich lady who lives at the top of the town. If I finish in time, we shall have a Christmas just the way Mother would have made it. I shall make you spiced cider and currant cakes, and you can have fresh tobacco for your pipe."

"And what would you be wanting, my girl?" he asked.

"Light in the house all the day long from the moment the sun rises to the second the night snatches it back," Claire said. "A crackling fire that never goes out. Candles that never burn down."

"I've never known such a girl for dreaming," her father said. "Especially when you have that wool running through your fingers."

Claire knit until she fell asleep. When her father rose in the morning, he shook her gently awake and gave her a cup of hot tea before he left the house.

By evening, Claire's back was sore and her legs stiff. Outside, the wind screamed up and down the narrow streets. Again, when her father came home he found Claire sitting in the dark and the cold. The only things moving in the dank, low room were his daughter's fingers and the dreams inside her head.

He slid the needles from her hands and carried her to bed.

At last, at the end of Christmas Eve day, the stockings were done. Claire laid all six of them together in a basket and lit a candle. When she saw for the first time the pictures she had painted with the wool, she clapped her hands in delight. On the stockings, flames flickered and candles burned and light streamed everlastingly through an open window. And here children were dancing around a bonfire, and there a jolly old man was ringing the bells of Christmas, and everybody was smiling and everybody was warm. Surely these were the best stockings she had ever made.

But it was growing late. She had to hurry if she was to deliver the stockings by six o'clock. The snow had been falling for hours, and she stopped for a minute to take shelter against the churchyard wall. All around her, people were rushing to finish their last Christmas errands. In one corner of the yard, she spotted a pile of rags, but just as she was about to start off again, the rags moved, and when she drew closer, she saw that it was a boy. He had a scrap of green scarf tied about his neck, and two naked feet stuck out from the bottom of his ragged trousers.

"Please," said a thin, reedy voice. "I am so cold. Have you nothing in your basket to warm my feet?"

Of course she had, but the stockings were spoken for. She hugged the basket close against her.

"Have you ever been cold?" he asked.

"I've rarely been warm," Claire answered.

"Then you know what it's like not to feel your feet."

She turned away and plodded up the steep hill, her head bowed against the wind. At the top, she looked back. Still the people were keeping their distance from the small, cold boy with feet he could no longer feel.

Perhaps the rich lady would not miss one pair of the stockings, Claire told herself as she hurried back down the hill. With the money from two pairs, she and her father would have enough for half a day of warm fires, an hour's worth of candles, a small pouch of new tobacco.

“Here, boy,” she said as she pulled two stockings over his toes, around his heels, and all the way up to his knees. His eyes grew wide with amazement.

“These stockings are magic,” he said. “Why, the heels of my feet are resting on the warm stones of a kitchen hearth and my toes are sunk in a puddle of hot summer mud.”

Claire smiled. “You’re dreaming my dreams, boy.” Then she saw that his skinny chicken-bone fingers were blue with cold. So she knelt down and pulled two of the stockings over his hands and up his arms to the elbows.

“These are even better,” he said. “I can feel the strong grasp of my father on my one hand and the tight circle of my mother’s fingers round the other, and it is certain that they will never let go of me again.”

Claire closed her eyes for a moment and heard the beat of her mother’s heart.

"You're dreaming my dreams, boy," she said again.

And as she rose, she saw how each separate strand of his snow-covered hair clung to its icy neighbor.

So she drew another stocking over his head. "One more for you, boy," she said. "Tell me of this one."

"This is truly the best of all. You have knit the music of bells into this stocking, and I can hear them ringing in all the corners of the town, up in the high streets and down in the low." He closed his eyes to listen.

"I must hurry now, boy, for I am already late."

But he gave no answer.

"I shall look for you when I come back," she called as she made her way up the steep cobbled hill. The last she saw of him was the foot of one wool stocking waving at her like a flag from the top of his head.

By the time Claire reached the big red house at the top of the hill, the bells of the church tower had long before rung six times. She knocked and knocked at the thick wooden door of the kitchen, and finally it was opened by the servant girl. Claire could hear music, and she could smell mince pies and mulled wine.

"Who is it?" called a voice from the other room.

"It's the stocking girl, ma'am."

"She's late," said the lady as she swept into the kitchen.

"And she's brought only one stocking," said the servant girl as she lifted it out of Claire's basket.

"I knit all six," said Claire, her voice trembling. "But there was a ragged boy freezing in the churchyard, and I—"

"Don't make up stories, girl," said the lady. She flung the one stocking back into the basket. "Be off, you lazy, lying thing. My servant will come down to collect the wool you owe me. Close the door," she barked at the servant girl. "The house is growing drafty."

Even after the door had been slammed shut, Claire could hear the music playing more loudly than before. She made her slow way down the snow-covered hill. Now there would be no fire to burn for Christmas Day, she thought, no spiced cider or cakes, no light in the house.

At the corner of the churchyard, she turned in to see the boy, but the rag pile was gone and the hollow his body had made in the snow had been smoothed by the wind. Perhaps someone had picked him up and carried him home to warm him by their fire. She hurried on, for her father had already started up the little lane, calling her name. She ran into his arms, and he carried her inside.

"Where have you been, my child? You are soaked through."

Claire was crying so hard she could not speak. He helped her change into dry clothes and hung her last stocking above the hearth.

"Our neighbors have given us the largest log from their woodpile," he said. "Our Christmas fire shall dry your stocking and warm your cold toes."

The fire crackled to life.

Together Claire and her father sat in the rocking chair while she told him the story of the boy.

"Those stockings were the prettiest and warmest I've ever made," Claire said. "But the children at the top of the hill would never have noticed. They already had music and mince pies and crackling fires."

"Your stockings are keeping one boy very warm," said her father.

"But I wanted a Christmas like the ones Mother made. And now it cannot be. No candles, no currant cakes, no tobacco for your pipe. And Mother is never coming back," Claire said at last.

"But she never left," her father whispered in Claire's ear. "Your mother is knit into you, just as your dreams are knit into the wool."

Lulled by the beat of her father's heart and the pop and crackle of the wood, Claire finally fell asleep.

When Claire opened her eyes the next morning, the room seemed brighter than usual. Her one stocking was still hanging above the fire, but it was bulging from bottom to top. She tiptoed over and lifted it down. Inside she found a pair of furry slippers and a pouch of tobacco, a bottle of cider, mulling spices, two currant cakes, and all the wool she owed to the lady in the house at the top of the hill. The best presents of all were tucked into the foot of the stocking. There Claire found candles and a bundle of kindling tied together with a scrap of green scarf.

"Father!" she cried, shaking him awake. "Come and see!"

She lit all the candles and the kindling and set a pot of cider to simmer. The fire hissed and the flames from the circle of candles danced up the walls until their tiny room seemed to grow bigger. She and her father stirred the cider and ate the currant cakes and made a merry Christmas.

All through the afternoon and into the evening, the candles burned, but the wax never dripped and the wicks never sputtered, and at the end of the day, the candles were each as tall as they had been in the morning. It was the same with the fire. It blazed merrily, but every time Claire looked, the pile of kindling was stacked as high as the moment she had first lit it. And so it would be for all the days and months and years ahead.

Word of Claire's magical light spread through the town. Soon she had more orders for her stockings than she could possibly fill, because the people believed it was the stockings themselves that had chased away the darkness in her house. The next Christmas and every one after that, people hung stockings above their hearths and made all sorts of wishes, for presents both large and small. And as happens with wishes, some came true and some did not.

From that day on, Claire's little house at the bottom of the lane glowed with a happy light both winter and summer. People were drawn to the house, and she made them welcome.

Claire could often be found rocking in her chair with her eyes closed, still dreaming her dreams and knitting them into the wool.

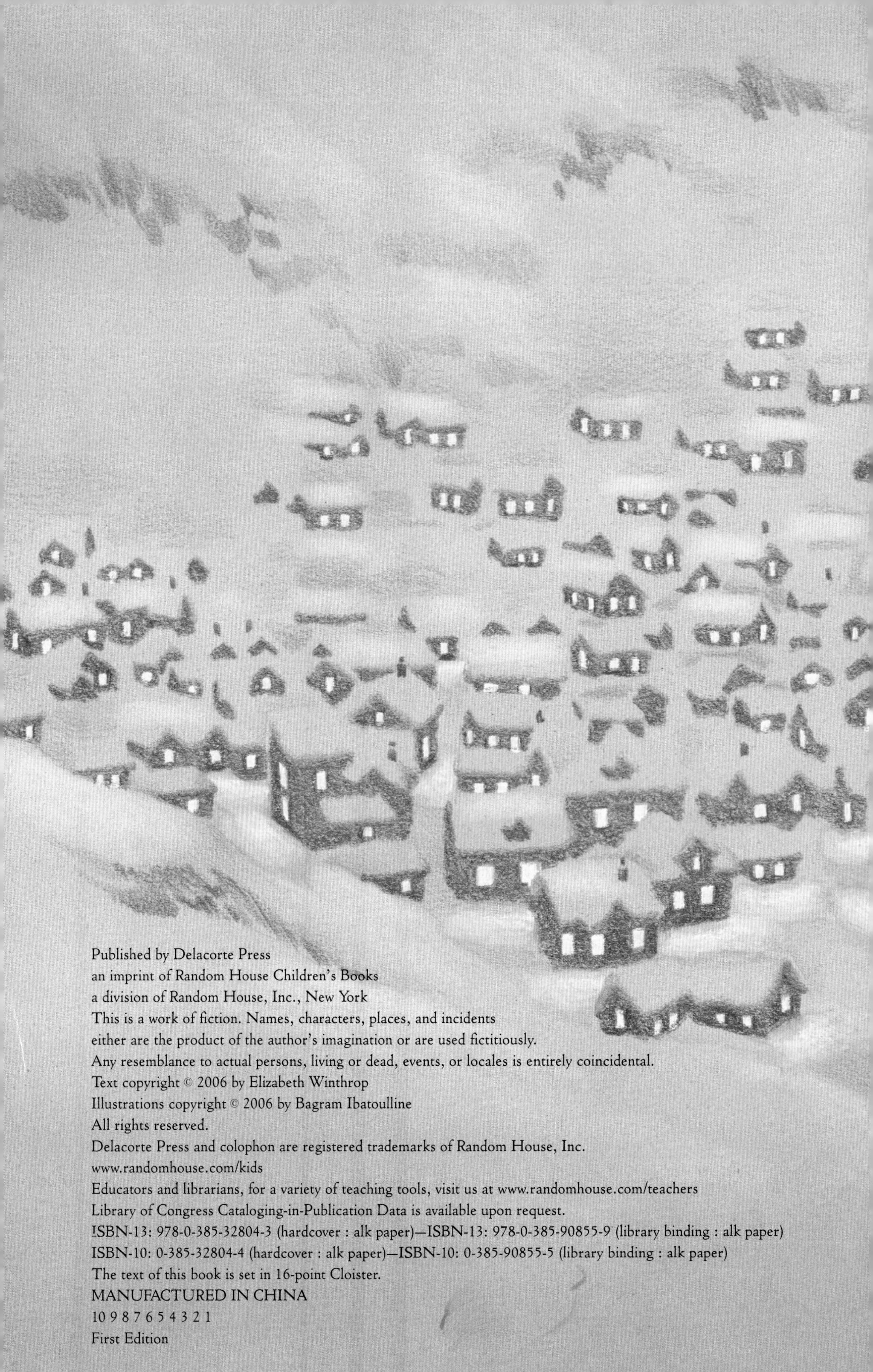

Published by Delacorte Press
an imprint of Random House Children's Books
a division of Random House, Inc., New York
This is a work of fiction. Names, characters, places, and incidents
either are the product of the author's imagination or are used fictitiously.
Any resemblance to actual persons, living or dead, events, or locales is entirely coincidental.

www.randomhouse.com/kids
Educators and librarians, for a variety of teaching tools, visit us at www.randomhouse.com/teachers
Library of Congress Cataloging-in-Publication Data is available upon request.
ISBN-13: 978-0-385-32804-3 (hardcover : alk paper)—ISBN-13: 978-0-385-90855-9 (library binding : alk paper)
ISBN-10: 0-385-32804-4 (hardcover : alk paper)—ISBN-10: 0-385-90855-5 (library binding : alk paper)
The text of this book is set in 16-point Cloister.
MANUFACTURED IN CHINA
10 9 8 7 6 5 4 3 2 1
First Edition